Succession

...

Succession

Art Norris

BRINDLE & GLASS

National Library of Canada Cataloguing in Publication Data
Norris, Art, 1963-
Succession / Art Norris.

ISBN 0-9732481-0-6
I. Title.
PS8577.O55S92 2003   C813'.6   C2003-911158-X

Cover photos: Molly Shier

Brindle & Glass Publishing
www.brindleandglass.com

1 2 3 4 5 06 05 04 03

PRINTED AND BOUND IN CANADA

For Kieran,
that we may have something to pass on to you.

◆ ◆ ◆

CONTENTS

• • •

Their farm was now hooked into the new waterline. They still had the well, though, and that was a good thing. The first winter after the pipeline was laid saw plenty of breaks and leaks. It was no wonder—new things never work perfectly the first time you try them, and it had been a very cold winter. The pipes froze and cracked. The district water co-op had its machines digging and growling from November through March, tracking and colouring the snow with soil and clay in a wide swath along their south pasture.

It ruined the view of the river valley.

Annie stood in the old bedroom that served as her studio and looked through the window at the mess left by the latest repairs to the waterline. It was so cold, all she could do was stay inside and look out. Look at that mess.

What she wanted to see was a clear sheet of white

snow, crumpled at the edges where the fences ran; the blue sky stretching from the mountains to forever; the hills stacking higher and higher from the valley on to the southwest. Before they'd sold the herd, she'd have seen some of the red-brown Guernsey cattle walking slowly across the pasture, heading for shelter.

But now there was a clay-coloured scar ripping across the foreground. Annie frowned and turned back to her painting. There were a couple of snapshots tacked to the top of the easel and most of an oil painting looking back at her—a neighbour's farm, photographed a month ago. She was almost finished the painting. She wanted to layer in a few more colours; the textures in the middle ground weren't quite right.

She glanced at the photographs and thought, It's good not to include the collapsed shed to the east of the house. She knew they were going to burn that heap of old boards and wood shingles soon, so she might as well edit it out of the painting now. She started mixing a blue-grey colour on the palette and forgot about the mangled pasture.

• • •

March and April came and went. The annual Cochrane Art Club spring show and sale was almost over. Annie's paintings had sold quickly. She was pleased. She thought they were good. After painting for thirty-five years, she hoped she'd learned something. Some strangers had gushed over her work, picking it out from among the two hundred pictures set up in the school gym. Annie blushed when she overheard them. They thought the paintings were underpriced. Annie's husband, James, would have laughed. He figured pictures were just something to stick on a wall to keep it from looking too blank. Paying more than twenty or thirty bucks for one was insane to him. But the canvas and frames and paints cost some money. So did the film and developing for the snapshots she used. And it took time to paint a good one.

And she was good at it, dammit.

Darn it.

Still, she felt a little bad when someone spent almost two hundred dollars on one of her pictures. It seemed a little wrong to take her share after the Art Club got its percentage. It was a lot of money to spend on something to put on a wall.

But the paintings sold, including the one of the Sherwin farm.

Annie sat at one of the rickety tables; she fingered the tissue-paper tablecloth and looked at the painting, which had a little green sticker indicating that it had been bought. She liked it. She really liked it. She had hesitated to bring it to the show, and now she was regretting that it was sold. It had been good to have it in her studio; if the Sherwins had still been living in the area she'd have liked to sell it to them. Then she could have seen it occasionally by dropping in for a visit. But it was sold now. She would find out who had bought it. It was good to know where her paintings went; she kept a list of purchasers.

The old Sherwin farm sits in the trough of a broad, shallow valley. The mountains can be seen even from the lowest point in the valley. It had taken Annie several attempts to get the perspective right, to translate the curves of the hills on the left and right onto the flat canvas. The first try just didn't work. The second version looked like prairie curled up at the sides like a sheet of folded paper. Eventually she got them to look like solid hills of the earth.

She still wasn't sure how she'd done it. If she could figure it out, she could do another one. But she wasn't sure.

This one she charged more for: $285. Maybe it wasn't enough. It was purchased less than an hour after the sale started.

She closed her eyes, and she could see the picture. She could see it in her mind. She kept a few paintings there. The image was clear and permanent in her memory; she could let the painting go now. It might be possible to paint another one like it.

Opening her eyes, she smiled and went to the coffee table to see if there was anyone to talk to.

• • •

A month later the country was turning green, tone by tone, day by day. The change was too quick to keep up with by painting. If you left the easel for a couple of days, the land would leap ahead of your picture. It was a time for taking photographs. Watching the process almost left Annie dizzy.

The grass was slowly overtaking the dug-up swath of the waterline. On a morning when it wasn't quite warm enough to sit on the back deck of the house, she walked across the yard with a cup of coffee to keep her hands warm. She watched the light on the pasture, on the valley and on the mountains. Again, she wished for a herd of red cattle. They looked so good in the green grass.

The day before, James had told her that Herb Sutherland was asking about renting the pasture. The grass was getting thick; it hadn't been grazed in two years, and a lot of dry grass in the fall could be a fire hazard. During the winter Annie and James had talked about renting it out. She knew it would be a good idea.

There was only one problem. Sutherland had a Charolais herd. White cows.

She imagined thirty off-white Charolais cattle in the pasture. It didn't look good. The bland, blanched cows had no richness, no substance in their colouring.

Annie had put up with the waterline all winter. She could rearrange some things in her paintings, but having drab cattle out in the pasture all summer, to be seen every day, was too much. She told James just that. He replied with that blank look of his, the one he wore every time he saw a new painting or watched the news.

Annie simply refused to have Charolais cattle in the pasture. That was the end of it, and James knew it.

"I don't want white cows here," she said.

He nodded and went to the phone to call Herb Sutherland.

• • •

The sun had risen high enough to shine into the valley. The light reflected up off the Bow River. The valley and the hills shone green. The coffee in her cup was cooling faster than Annie could drink it; she stood holding the mug with both hands. She closed her eyes and smiled. Some things can't be painted. Some things are just for inside. Other things are on a larger scale. She could refuse to paint those white cows, and keeping them off the farm was the same kind of thing. If James didn't understand that . . . well, he didn't understand her paintings either.

It really is a beautiful part of the world, she thought. Sometimes you just have to do what you have to do to keep it that way.

This is foolish, he thought. I'll burn as red as rosehips in this sun. Al peeled off his T-shirt, the stretched cotton neck catching on the brim of his cap and the cups of his hearing protectors. He stood up, dropped the sweaty shirt onto the tractor seat and sat down again. The steering wheel stayed more or less in position through most of this operation and started to swing to the left just as Al was sitting down.

His arms were red and brown from where his gloves covered his wrists to the bottom seams of his T-shirt sleeves. The skin was streaked with fresh dirt and one broad scrape inflicted the day before when a wrench had slipped off of a bolt head. Thus anointed by field and machine, Al drove the tractor and hay mower along a rectangular, spiral course.

It had been six years since he last drove a tractor on this field. He liked it then. He had forgotten how much he liked it. The highest points in the field were ridges in the southwest and northwest corners. The land sloped from these points to the east end, with an uneven trough snaking from the southwest to the middle. With sixteen rounds done, the wide outer margin of the field was neatly tied down by a long, metre-wide rope of cut hay.

It was past noon. Al had been on the tractor since eight o'clock. His lunch was in a canvas sack at the southeast corner. He rolled in the tractor seat, easy with the bumps as he mowed along the north side of the field, heading east. He had to remind himself to look back at intervals to see that the swath was even and clean. The sickle was cutting well; no lines of uncut hay were standing in its wake. Allowing himself confidence in the machine, Al stood on the treads and watched, and saw the land roll past him. The curves and angles changed with his movement. The topography gradually wrapped up and behind him. The parallel lines of the swath and the uncut middle of the field wavered in the heat. Al was at the wet point of some calligrapher's pen, trailing a Celtic scroll across a twenty-four acre patch of wrinkled earth.

The hard regularity of fencelines and machined swaths were uncomfortable on the smooth curves of the land, but the arbitrary square of the cleared field held its own grace. The land was comfortable enough under the rule-straight lines of human geometry. Al and the tractor crawled along at four miles per hour and the field and sky filled the whole of Al's vision. And Al felt good.

A decal on the dashboard reminded Al to run the tractor's diesel engine for a few minutes, to circulate the coolant, before shutting it down. He put the mower out of gear and let the tractor idle while he examined the sickle, checking each metal section bolted to the cutting bar. They were fine; nothing was loose or seriously chipped. It was like practicing dentistry on an iron shark. The knife guards, pointing forward and more wicked-looking than the sickle they surrounded, were all tight and whole.

Al had stopped in the southeast corner near his lunch. He shut down the engine and hung his orange hearing protectors over the steering wheel. Standing beside the tractor, he listened to the mower settling on its hydraulics and to the light rustling noises in the uncut hay. Wind. Mice. Birds.

Windrows of hay dictate a weird stride for crossing a field: left – right – hop – left – right – hop. Al aimed for his food and ran like a crippled hurdler over the cut hay. At the corner he stopped and stretched. He turned till he was facing the sun. He slowly lowered his arms, then opened his eyes and squinted in the light.

Across the fence was a mixed herd of Holsteins and Herefords ambling from grazing to the dugout. They too were thirsty. Al pulled a bottle of Big Rock Traditional Ale from his sack. The night before, after supper, Al had built his lunch: two thick sandwiches— one of ham, tomato, and lettuce; the other of cheese, onions, and lettuce. He ate first half of one, then half of the other. He opened the beer in the intermission between sandwiches. A cow looked up from thirty yards away at the sound of the air being released from the bottle. She looked at Al, then continued on to the dugout. Al raised his bottle to her and drank.

The heifer ambled on. Her body swayed slightly and her muscles rippled under her hide. The black and white patches of her fur wrapped around each other like the unlikely continents and seas of a mythical world. A misshapen globe, a multistomached living earth, temporary home to some pesky flies, on her way to a gathering of the planets.

The heifer belonged to Tim Jones, a neighbouring dairy farmer, and to Tim, the heifer's markings would be as familiar as a friend's face. Al doubted his own ability to distinguish her from another Holstein. He tried to see a pattern in her markings, some familiar shape to refer to. But her markings were no more symmetrical or memorable or sensible than, say, the surface of Earth at first glance. Who, Al wondered, remembers a first sight of Earth?

He took another couple of drinks of his dark beer, then bit into the last half of his cheese sandwich. He lay back onto the wild native grasses and stared through living and dead willow branches. He chewed. Clouds covered about a third of the blue sky.

There was a rock group from Ontario called The Continental Drift, or Somebody's Name and The Continental Drift. Weird band, did mostly satirical songs. Great name, anyway. Continental drift. As Al stretched out on the grass and devoured his sandwiches he thought of the pictures or maps of the Earth at multimillion year intervals, showing the movement of land masses from one supercontinent—is that what they call it?—through a tearing stage to gradual separation. Africa turning its back on Asia. North America crawling west to complete its divorce from Europe. Maybe that explains the steady buildup of trade between the Far East and North America, he thought: commerce following the intention of geological evolution.

With a final bite of ham and bread in his mouth, Al reached with the hand that wasn't holding the beer and pulled an apple out of the canvas sack. He sat up enough to take another drink. He held the beer on his tongue before slowly swallowing it, then took another mouthful. He lay back and turned the apple until he had a grip on it that felt right in his hand. He just lay there without biting.

Two small flies were darting in confused rectangles an arm's reach above Al's head. He felt some other insect on his cheek, exploring his stubble. He let it crawl. It had no idea what he was thinking about. Al smiled unconsciously and the bug paused when the surface under it moved and formed a dimple one antenna-length ahead of it. It crawled forward until its six legs were each standing on a separate whisker.

Al bit into his apple. The insect left.

Al felt the slight sensation of movement deep below him, rolling under legs and hips, his back, his head. Is it the drift of continents? he wondered. Maybe it's the planet turning, or the slow seasonal wiggle of the poles toward and away from the sun.

The puff of a breeze tugged at the grass and leaves around him. Al bit into the apple again and stretched out. He tilted his head to the left, then to the right. His neck made a cracking sound and Al felt a release of tension in his neck and back. He lay motionless and ate his apple.

He sat up to swallow and found he'd finished his

beer. There were still two cookies in his bag. He took them to eat later. Looking up, he saw that the clouds were farther east and each one had changed shape in some minor but discernible way. Al hadn't realized that he'd been noticing the shapes of the clouds.

He stood, and his legs felt too light. A yellowish tint covered the hayfield and details of even the far side of the field had clarity. To the west a heat shimmer rippled the air above the road, just beyond the fence. The breeze sounded on the hairs above Al's ears.

A scream was launched into the silence high above him, and Al looked up to see two hawks circling. He smiled and started back to the tractor. "Watch it, guys," he said aloud to the mice and gophers. A gopher chirped from a hole a few yards to his left. "Don't say I didn't warn you."

◆ ◆ ◆

The afternoon rolled by under the wheels of the tractor. The mower cut cleanly; the field was at its smoothest in the middle. Round by round, the area of uncut hay became smaller. As he neared the centre, Al stopped mowing the east and west edges and lifted the mower on its hydraulics for a wide arc around the ends rather than trying to cut increasingly sharp corners.

He was moving east, with two rounds to go, when a family of grouse trotted out from the hay in front of him. A mother and five chicks glanced in the direction of the noise and started to run from it. They kept pace with the tractor, staying about ten yards ahead. Even in their panic they held to an orderly single file. The mother turned every few feet to look back, and wobbled as gracelessly as her chicks. Al smiled. "Sorry!" he called. "Don't worry. I won't run you over."

As they passed the edge of the uncut hay, the mother took to the air and cleared the first windrow by a couple of feet. She shifted in a moment from a Charlie Chaplin waddle to fluid flight. Her chicks followed one by one. Once they moved from feet to wings, none of them looked funny or silly or cute.

The hawk appeared suddenly, enormous as it dropped below the upper horizon of Al's hat brim. Its speed and movement seemed wrong in the first instant of its arrival. Al stomped on the clutch and the brakes as though that might stop the hawk as well as the tractor.

Just as the last young bird rose to Al's eye level, the hawk intercepted it. The birds hit the ground together. A feather was left floating in the air at the point where they had collided above the ground. The wind lifted it and blew it past the tractor. The hawk opened its beak, but its scream was drowned by the diesel engine. It shook its wings like a big man shrugging into an overcoat, then left the ground with fine drops of blood falling from the dead bird in its talons.

Al watched the hawk until it ducked around a clump of poplars.

• • •

Al and his uncle Herb had lasagna that evening. After eating and before the water boiled for tea, they discussed the day.

"How'd it go with the baling?"

"Fine."

A pause.

"How was the mower?"

"No problems."

"Good to get that field cut."

"Everything went well."

"Good. Johnny said he'd come over with the stacker tomorrow. He picks up bales faster than I can make them." Johnny was a retired farmer with plenty of equipment and an unretired urge to do field work when the weather was good.

The water boiled; Al poured it over the tea bags in the pot.

"A hawk killed a young grouse. Right in front of the tractor this afternoon."

"Startled you, eh?"

"Yeah. And then some."

"Yeah. You see a lot of things out in the fields if you spend any kind of time in them."

◆ ◆ ◆

After the morning chores and breakfast, with the coffee half drained, they plotted the day.

"So you want me to cut that field across the highway?"

"Yeah." Pause. "I don't want you to get too far ahead of me. But the weather is supposed to hold. Yeah, take the mower across the road."

"Okay."

"You know Bert Dunne and his boy are living in a trailer over there, in the next field."

"Yeah, I remember."

"They might offer you lunch. Or they might not."

"I've got my own, anyway."

"Good."

They went to their tractors.

◆ ◆ ◆

Al waited at the highway for the commuter traffic to thin out enough for him to cross. FARM EQUIPMENT CROSSING, as the sign said. The sign had been ploughed into the ditch sometime in the years since Al had moved to Vancouver. Al looked at it but wasn't able to read the words on the sign from his angle. Birds could see it shining in the sun. Occasionally a duck would see the reflection from a bad angle and investigate, hoping for water.

Al thought, A highway is a dangerous place for a duck.

Finally, just after a vanload of frantically waving children had smiled their blessing on Al and his Cool Machine, he crossed the asphalt and entered the field.

Al pulled on the rope tied to a spring-loaded pin, then jerked his foot off the clutch. The tractor jumped forward and the mower yawed into field position. Al let the rope go and the pin socked into the appropriate hole. He threw the lever to engage the power takeoff and the mower clattered into action. Circular, back-and-forth, and up-and-down movements of metal parts signalled their functions in polyrhythms, improvising a mesh of 2/2 and 6/8 time.

It was a big field on high ground overlooking the Bow River valley. The city was visible over Al's left shoulder as he travelled west in a clockwise circuit. The downtown towers hung on the horizon, blurred by exhaust fumes.

After three rounds, a line of upright grass appeared behind the mower. Al stopped and disengaged the PTO and dropped the throttle. He pushed the hydraulic lever and rolled the tractor back away from the uncut hay. Al found the broken sickle section and swept the dirt and grass away from it. He frowned at it, with little effect, and pulled some wrenches from a compartment at the back of the machine. The last time he'd operated the mower, the sections were attached to the sickle bar with rivets. At some point the rivets had been replaced by small bolts. This made the process of changing the sections in the field a lot easier. Still, it had been a few years since Al had done it and there was some banging and bleeding and swearing involved before the broken section was removed and the new one installed.

Satisfied with the repair, he lay for a moment on the ground, looking up past the machine at the sky and the clouds. He grabbed the front bar of the mower and shuffled out from under the machine. He'd left the tractor running, and now he noticed again the fast, steady rhythm of the engine that had droned into the background while he had been working on the sickle.

The tractor, the mower, and Al rolled along for the

rest of the morning without a problem. On the last round before lunch, on the north side of the field, a coyote loped out of the tall grass and stopped fifty yards ahead of Al. The coyote stood, looking over his shoulder at the tractor, then started trotting along the windrows. It didn't look right to Al. The coyote's hind end had too much vertical movement. Al slowly gained ground on him and saw that the coyote's left rear leg was scrawny and hanging useless from the hip.

The coyote returned to the high grass before Al reached the corner.

Al stopped the tractor and walked to where his lunch sat under his jacket. Someone was standing just beyond the fence. He guessed—and he was right—that it was Barry Dunne.

Al called to him, "Hi, guy! How goes it?" Al hadn't seen or spoken to Barry in over ten years, but they had never been close enough in the past to need any lengthy greetings now.

"Not bad," said Barry. "Want a beer?"

"Sure. Thanks." Al twisted off the bottlecap and dropped it into his lunch bag. Barry was already well started on his drink. He crossed through the fence without spilling and Al pulled a sandwich out of its plastic wrap. He offered half to Barry, who shook his head. Al balanced his beer on a fencepost. "I'd better have some of this before I drink more beer. Empty stomach, you know."

"Beer loves an empty stomach."

"Too well. It's been a while, eh?"

"It sure has."

"Still working at the garage?"

"Yeah. No. Different garage."

"Oh, yeah."

"You still playing in that band?"

Which one? thought Al. "Taking a break from the music," he said. "Last band I was in, I left it in the spring."

"You play guitar, don't you?"

"Bass, mostly."

"Right." Barry finished his beer and opened another bottle. "I used to play drums."

"I remember. In school."

"Yeah. Not much anymore, though."

"No, eh?" Al drank a bit more from his beer. He felt a little light-headed. Better go slow on this bottle.

"No," said Barry. "No one to play with, really. Not since high school."

"Yeah. That's too bad."

"Is that why you moved to Vancouver? No one around here to jam with?"

"Well, maybe. Mostly I just wanted to go. Then I started with a band when I got there."

"Yeah? What was it called? Your band?"

What was it called? Al couldn't remember. "It was a country-rock outfit." What was the name? "It changed names a couple of times. Only lasted seven or eight months."

"You can't remember the name?"

"Well, no."

"Really?"

"Really. I don't remember." Barry didn't seem able to believe it. "You see, bands start up and fold, or change members. Change names. Disappear. They aren't like families, you know. There's often more reasons to move along than there are to stay with a group."

"Really."

"Yeah. The people don't get along. The music sometimes isn't all that good. You get bored. The band can't get gigs after a while. A band needs something special, or unusual or I don't know what, to hold together. And luck, too."

"You played with a lot of bands?"

"Yeah. A lot. Sometimes only for a night or two." God, how many bands had it been?

"How many?"

"God, I don't know. Dozens." Hundreds? Al finished his sandwich and drank down a large mouthful of beer.

"That many?"

"That many."

"Groupies?"

"What? Oh, groupies. Sometimes." Al didn't like the expression, and he didn't use it often. "Not anymore."

"Got a steady woman now."

"Yeah. Betty. What about you? You got a girlfriend?"

"No, not me. Not for a while now." Barry took a long swig. His beer belly started to escape from his shirt as he scratched his head with his free hand. "No, I'm a free man."

"I try, in my way, to be free."

"Yeah, well, here's to ya." Barry raised his bottle.

"And here's to you."

Barry pulled a third beer for himself. "Drink much?"

"Not as much as I used to."

"C'mon, you're a rock and roll animal, aren't you?"

"Once in a while. Get headaches, though."

"Drugs?"

"Used to. You aren't a narc, are you?"

Barry laughed. "Get real! No, really. Do you play better when you're stoned? They say you play better when you're stoned."

"Do they?"

"Yeah, you know, frees the creative juices, shit like that."

"Maybe it does."

"So, do you?"

"Play stoned. I used to, once in a while."

"Did you play better?"

"I'll never know. When I did, I was always too stoned to notice a difference."

Barry laughed. "So. Are you around for long?"

"Until haying's done."

"So I'll be seeing you around."

"Yeah, for a while. Then I'm back to the coast."

"And to Betty."

"You bet."

"Well, I won't keep you from your tractor."

"That's all right."

"See you later."

"You bet. Take 'er easy."

"You bet." Barry turned and walked back to his trailer. Al watched him go, then pulled out a muffin. As he finished his lunch, he looked up and saw the coyote sitting beside the tractor. The coyote watched Al come across the swaths of hay, then yawned, stood up, and limped back into the high grass.

After another hour of cutting, Al noticed that

more and more tufts of grass were surviving the mower. The sections along the sickle bar were getting dull. The coyote appeared once more as Al shifted the mower into road position, and watched as the big, loud machine left his hunting grounds. There was less cover for him now, but there was also less cover for the mice, moles, and gophers.

Back in the farmyard, Al hosed the dirt off the sickle, unbolted it, and pulled it out using a length of smooth fencewire looped around the end. He lay the sickle on the workbench. A fresh, sharp sickle lay along the opposite wall. Al's uncle walked in from the field as Al was shoving the sickle into place. Herb leaned over the front of the machine and guided the sickle with a hammer, preventing it from jamming against the guards. He handed Al the wrenches he needed to bolt the new sickle onto the drive arm. With the last few turns of the wrench, he asked Al, "How's it going?"

"Not bad." What was the name of that band? "Blades just getting dull."

"Not surprising."

How many bands?

"You're way ahead of the baler, anyway."

Playing stoned.

"Well, I'll sharpen this tomorrow. You might as

well take it easy for the rest of the day. Sleep in tomorrow, too, eh?"

"Yeah, okay. I will." Al looked up through the machine, past his uncle, to the clouds. "Thanks."

• • •

Al showered. He shaved and dressed, and put on deodorant for the first time in days. He ate a cookie and phoned Betty. The answering machine picked up after three rings and his own voice asked for a message. It was the same voice that kept asking him, What was that band's name?

He told the answering machine the time he called, then subtracted an hour for the difference in time zones. He said he was going out and would call again later. He found his wallet and keys and headed to Calgary, looking for voices other than his own.

The farm lay on the 1A highway, less than ten minutes' drive from the city. It was closer than it had been when Al was growing up in the district. A golf course surrounded by a thick wall of condominiums now sat on the northeast corner of the intersection of the highway and Bearspaw Road. More houses had been built all along the highway in recent years. None of this surprised Al. He turned on his radio, but it was still tuned to a Vancouver station and played only static. After a moment of hiss, he turned it off.

A truck was parked off the highway with a large sign: FRESH BC FRUIT. Al pulled up to it. Other customers were picking through the baskets. Al went straight to the cherries and scooped up a couple of handfuls. The vendor made change and chattered.

"Your van?" He pointed at Al's Chevy. "With the BC plates?"

"That's right."

"Where ya from?"

"Vancouver."

"Big town. Too much town for my liking."

"You aren't alone in that."

"I know. I know it. What do you have there . . . cherries. Don't I know it. Vancouver big enough for you?"

"Yeah, I like it fine."

"Well that's what counts. Headed into town?"

Al hesitated as he looked over to the city. The roofs of the newer part of town rippled in the heat rising off the asphalt. Two lines of street lights came over the hill with the highway, probing like antennae.

"No, not today. Just out for a drive."

"Sure thing. Take it easy."

"You too."

Al took it easy, driving a serpentine route of back-roads back to the farm. The air held smells of earth and hay. It filled the van as Al drove through the farm-land, slowing to read the mailboxes. He rhymed some lines for a potential song and hoped to recall them later. He stopped at the crest of a hill and got out to scan a circle around himself, centering himself in the landscape.

Hunger took him back to the farm. His uncle had gone out, according to a note on the kitchen table, to eat and "buy supplies." Al ate leftovers.

He pulled his amp and bass guitar out of the basement and sat up on the deck. He tuned by ear and checked, unnecessarily, using an electronic tuner. He turned up the volume and walked about on the deck for a few moments, then played a slow scale in A. He touched a harmonic at the end of the scale and opened his eyes. The limping coyote had crossed the highway and was sitting on a low hill in the back pasture, look-ing at him.

Al played. He played bass lines from country tunes. He adapted lead riffs from old and new rock songs. He played parts of melodies. He played a waltz. For an hour he played. The sun sank to the mountains and backlit the coyote. Finally, Al played a particularly tasty bass lick from a Paul Simon song.

The coyote yipped twice into the silence after the Simon riff. Al smiled and watched him turn toward the highway and limp away.

"You got it, pal," he said. He turned off the amp and carried it back into the living room, then dialed his number in Vancouver.

Al left another message on the answering machine, then he tore a couple of pages of music manuscript paper from a pad and started writing Betty a letter.

Johnny put away his ball-peen hammer. It had its own hook on a pegboard above the bench. Indelible ink traced an accurate outline of the tool on the board; every tool with an ascribed resting place on the board had a similar outline.

Johnny replaced his pliers and clamps into their labelled drawers. He took a whisk broom and a dustpan down and swept up a few flakes of paint, none bigger than a fingernail clipping. He swept up the floor around the workbench. A can of dark green paint sat on the bench beside his restored metal mailbox, but he wasn't ready to paint over his faded last name. That would be the final touch; he had more work to do first.

A small electric concrete mixer slurped and clattered in the corner. He had set it up earlier so the mix would be ready for when he had finished his other preparations. Johnny took the big old mailbox over and set it down, door upwards, on a tarp in front of the concrete mixer. He stabilized it with cinder blocks, then carefully poured the concrete mixture into the mailbox to a depth of about two inches. He turned around and picked up a brand new, smaller mailbox. He had removed the flap from the front as soon as he had brought it home.

The new mailbox fit into the old one with an inch to spare in each direction. Johnny lined it up and pressed it down into the wet cement. He tapped it down until the front edge was flush with the opening of the old mailbox. He quickly slid one-inch-wide slats of wood down the sides, top, and bottom of the new mailbox to wedge it into place, then poured concrete in to surround the new mailbox. Johnny took a piece of rebar and tamped it into the concrete to fill any air pockets. He used a trowel to scoop a little more in and then to smooth it off with room for the flap to close easily.

The little bit of excess concrete was poured out onto a piece of scrap cardboard, and Johnny dragged the cement mixer out into the rain and sluiced it out onto the grass.

With everything cleaned and put away, there was still an hour until his usual lunch. On a rainy day, though, Johnny figured that he could take more time to eat.

• ◆ •

Johnny stood in his rain slicker and met the mailman
at the road, then sorted through his mail on his way
back to his house. He dropped the junk mail into the
incinerator—an oil barrel with the top sliced off and
wire mesh sitting on top. He went inside and slipped
the bills into a slot in his desktop organizer. He sat
down with the local paper and a flyer advertising used
farm equipment. After reading everything pertinent or
interesting, Johnny dozed upright in his armchair.

Never used to sleep in the middle of the day, he
thought, as he twitched himself awake. Must be the
weather. Must be getting older. I am getting old.

Seventy-two years of momentum roused Johnny
from his chair. He opened the fridge and was reaching
for some leftover soup to reheat for lunch. He stopped
and reconsidered. For breakfast, he had eaten only a
bowl of cornflakes. It hadn't been enough, and Johnny
was feeling the need for a proper breakfast. Four slices
of bacon hit the griddle. Four slices of bread stood
ready in the toaster. Coffee started perking. Butter and
jam, salt and pepper were set in ranks on the kitchen
table. Bacon was prodded and turned. The oven was
switched on to 175 degrees. The plunger on the toaster
went down. The four slices of bacon were pulled from

the pan like netted fish. They landed on the plate in the oven. Three eggs were cracked and dropped into the grease, spitting at each other. The toast was buttered and stacked beside the bacon. Finally, the eggs were retrieved from the grease and flopped onto the plate.

Johnny sat down to enjoy the same breakfast he'd been enjoying almost every day of his life since his early childhood.

Half an hour later, Johnny threw up in the bathroom.

◆ ◆ ◆

The next morning, Johnny enjoyed his breakfast again, with no violent reaction.

He went out to his shop, loaded the cement mixer into his pickup truck, and filled it. He plugged it in and set it running.

Johnny rolled his welding rig to within reach of the workbench where the new mailbox sat. He secured a five-foot section of railroad rail to the mailbox with a system of ropes and load straps. The bolts he'd mounted on the mailbox fit snugly down inside the side channels of the rail. He paused for a moment, trying to remember where he'd found the rail. He had a habit of picking up things that might be useful, and eventually they usually were. Where the rail came from, he couldn't remember. He shook his head and dropped the welder's mask down in front of his eyes.

Johnny took his time. He did a thorough job. The concrete mailbox and its bolts were cleanly and squarely bonded to the rail. He leaned a plank against the lowered tailgate of the truck to serve as a ramp, then used a block-and-tackle to draw the mailbox into the truck.

Two days before, when he retrieved the bent-up mailbox from the ditch, Johnny had dug out the old post and widened the hole. He now backed up to it, keeping as far onto the narrow shoulder of the road as possible. He turned on the four-way flashers and the radio and set to work. The flashers ticked under the talk radio show.

Johnny lined up the plank with the mailbox on it and pushed it out along the tailgate. He kept the rope on the mailbox and used it for control as the plank tipped down to the opening of the post hole. The rail jabbed the hole like a hypodermic needle. Johnny heaved up the plank and arced it to near vertical. The rail dropped the rest of the way into position. As he worked, Johnny ignored the commercials, then listened to the news. He hopped down and wiggled and turned the mailbox to face the right direction. Satisfied, he lined up the cement mixer and tipped it. Concrete poured like porridge into the hole; the news reader recited the litany of the usual outrages of politics and crime. Someone had been killed in an accident; some famous person wasn't. Johnny kept one hand on the mixer and used a short-handled shovel to direct concrete around the rail. When the hole was almost full, he dropped the shovel and used a broken broom handle to tamp down the mixture around the rail.

After more commercials came the afternoon sports panel. No hockey in the summer, and a bit early for football. Baseball talk. Johnny could listen to this. He dropped the broom handle beside the shovel and poured the rest of the concrete around the base of the rail. Baseball had been his game when he was younger. He still watched it. Of course, half the talk was about salaries and contracts. The business, if not the game, had changed. The players were bigger and stronger. The equipment was changing. Aluminum bats, of course. Finally, he nailed rough boards around the rail to disguise it. At a distance, or at high speed, it would look like a regular wooden fencepost.

Johnny snorted. Wonder what kind of bat was used on the mailbox. Three times in three months, some young jerks had driven along, swinging at all the older mailboxes up the road from the highway. Once they'd even stopped to tip the big green one at the entrance to the new development.

Aluminum or wood?

Johnny checked the plumb and level of the post one last time and loaded his tools into the truck.

When I was a young jerk, Johnny thought, we only used wooden bats on mailboxes.

Bits of food were drying and crusting on the plates. The dishes were stacked up beside the sink. Dinner had stretched out over an hour and a half. Everyone had carried that second cup of coffee, or that third beer, onto the deck with their conversation.

God, these people can talk! Betty thought. They must store up their words, alone all day on their tractors and machines. Open them up and out it comes.

Betty tried not to think about the stack of dirty dishes solidifying in the kitchen. She liked to get things like that out of the way. Get them done and carry on with other things. At the moment, however, she was still getting a kick out of watching Al with his Uncle Herb, his brother-in-law Ray, and a wiry old neighbour named Johnny. And she was damned if she was going to fall into any typically female role too easily. The dishes would still be there when the farming jargon became unintelligible.

This was her first visit to the farm. In three years of living with Al, she'd heard him refer to this place and these people many times, but seldom with detailed descriptions or complete stories. It was the place he'd come from, in the past tense. He would go for months without talking about it at all.

Then he went for a month hardly talking about anything at all.

It was when he was playing bass in a classic rock band. He'd been with them for four months. Steady work, steady money, steady stagnation. Betty knew he hated that kind of gig. A lot of the songs were good, but constant repetition slowly destroyed the fire and passion that gave birth to the music in the first place.

Al still had fire and passion, but they were no longer going with him to gigs. It was no wonder he was grumpy and silent. He was making his living by killing his music and beating up on songs he'd spent his teenage years listening to on truck radios.

Betty didn't know what to do, if anything. She started to play more current tapes at home, or the much older or more obscure music in Al's collection.

That helped a bit.

Al started talking about the farm again in March.

He told more stories. He filled in more details. He'd pick up his six-string and play in the afternoons, avoiding the band's repertoire.

He quit the band in May. Al had trudged out to his van with his instrument and amplifier, got to the bar in plenty of time, plugged in, tuned up, and ran through a few scales, just as he always did. He hardly said a word to the other members of the band. They didn't notice; Al had been talking less and less with them over time.

They played through their repertoire exactly as they always did. Al had one beer after each set. After each beer he went outside to walk up and down the alley, then he would return in time to check his tuning and be ready for the next set.

The band went onstage for its last set. They played the set list exactly as they always had. Al played by rote, calculating how much he was being paid on a per-note basis. It wasn't enough.

The music passed him by like a train deliberately missed, until they came to the end of "Proud Mary." He played his part dutifully. He moved around on the tiny stage enough to give the impression of actually being involved. He scarcely noticed the sound of his A-string breaking. It registered in his consciousness as pop on a vinyl record. What brought him back to the moment was the moisture dripping over his left eyelid. It took him a few moments to interpret the warmth and stickiness of the liquid and the colour of the drops on his hand as being his own blood.

Al did nothing to stop the flow of blood. He wiped some out of his eye, turned to the guitar player, and said, "I think I better go have this dealt with."

"Yeah, no kidding, man. You okay?"

"It missed my eye."

"Holy shit, I mean . . . I never seen a bass string snap like that."

"Me neither," said Al as he turned off his amp and unplugged his bass. Then he stopped and looked around at the bar and at the band. Every detail of the place and every face impaled itself on his memory. He dragged the case for his instrument out from under the drum riser and snapped it open. "I've never seen one snap before."

He packed up his instrument, stood up, and said, "That's it for me. I quit. See you around." He walked out with his gear and drove himself home.

Betty was surprised to hear the door open; she wasn't expecting Al for another hour. She also wasn't expecting him to be covered in blood.

Once she got over her first two or three reactions, she loaded Al back into the van and hauled him over to a clinic. They waited a relatively short time, and the doctor kept asking how it happened. Al's story didn't change, and the doctor gave up.

After they got home, Betty looked at the stitches in the odd, curving scar, then went to the fridge for a bottle of wine. She poured herself a glass, then offered one to Al. She looked at him again and went to a bookcase. She looked through some of Al's books and came back with a large-format book, *Jazz Scales for the Bass Guitar.* She flipped it open, looked up at Al, and said, "That's it."

"That's what?"

"This," she said. She turned the book around for him to see. "The shape of your scar. It's a bass clef."

Al looked at the symbol, then at a mirror. He looked back at Betty. He raised his eyebrows and she started to laugh. "Now you've turned it into a question mark."

"Is that what they mean by a quizzical expression?"

• • •

Quitting the band was even more of a relief for Betty than it was for Al. He'd actually been able to save some money over the winter, so the rent was still going to get paid. Betty would come home from the

CONCERNING U-JOINTS

restaurant to find that more and more little jobs around the apartment were getting done. Dinner became a small, creative feast most evenings. Al was playing a lot more music on his guitars at night. "The Eagles," he said, "have flown."

He kept telling stories of his family's farm. Betty tried to piece together a picture of the place and the people from Al's anecdotes and references. When she asked a question to clarify how some person was related to the others, or what some farming term meant, she'd often get the beginning of an answer that swerved off into another story. She did figure out that Al's sister, Rhonda, had married quite young. She and her husband Ray took over the farm after their parents retired for good. "They retired once," Al explained, "by selling the dairy herd and buying beef cows. Then they retired again and moved to Arizona." There was a bachelor uncle on another farm down the road as well. Betty lost track of who was who when the talk ran to neighbours. When it became too obscure, or repetitive, she started tuning out Al's chopped-up narrative.

At the beginning of June, during the fourth telling of a story about a one-horned bull, Betty surprised herself by saying, "Are you wanting to go back to the farm?"

Al didn't pick up on the irritation in her voice. He raised his eyebrows and thought about it. Betty raised her eyebrows and thought about it, too. She realized that returning to the farm would be good for Al. She also realized, in that moment, that she liked the idea of the farm as a part of Al's history, but the present reality of it disturbed her. She had her own images of the farm, the people, and the Bearspaw district from Al's stories. That was fine, but the idea of being there, meeting the people, made her nervous. She didn't know why.

"You can, you know," she said. "I probably can't get the time off work, but it sounds like you want to go."

Al thought about it, and they talked about it. Al phoned his uncle and arranged to show up in Bearspaw in late June.

And so he went. Betty felt nervous about it all again when the time came. The nervousness quickly fell away and grumpiness filled in its space. For a few days she was grumpy about the things Al hadn't cleaned up or put away. The bathroom—he never really cleans the bathroom. Guitar picks in all sorts of places.

Then she was grumpy about the things that he always did, things that weren't getting done with him gone. Dinner became boring.

The grumpiness passed. She missed him. Betty enjoyed having the place to herself for a while, but an absence with Al's name was shadowing her around the apartment.

They talked on the phone.

He wrote her a letter.

She'd never had a letter from him before. They were both living in Vancouver when they met. They could always phone each other or talk; there was no need to write letters. Seeing her name in his handwriting on a thick envelope made her cry. She read the letter and cried, then made a huge mug of hot chocolate and read it again.

She called her best friend and talked for an hour.

Betty arranged for a week off from work and took a Greyhound to Calgary at the end of July.

• • •

Al's old neighbours and family seemed to accept her fairly easily, and Betty found relaxing among them to be easier than she had expected. They all laughed the same way, the way Al laughed. And here she was, laughing with a Big Rock Pale Ale in her hand, surrounded by people with sunburnt, beefy arms, on a deck with a view of fields, foothills, and mountains.

By God, you can see every damned tree on those mountains and they're fifty miles away. This is what Al meant when he talked about the light in Alberta. And the sky. The phrase "big sky country" had seemed silly to her before. Not anymore.

Betty chose a spot on the bench that gave her a view of the mountains. She forgot about the dishes.

Al and his brother-in-law were talking about the evolution of the automated stacker. Al had missed a few years in the machine's progress, so he was asking most of the questions.

The old neighbour, Johnny, left his analysis of the Americanization of the CFL to join in on the stacker discussion.

"It's not the big stuff that impresses me," he said. "The overall shape of the machine, the conveyor chains, the spikes—that stuff is fairly obvious—"

"How else would you design it?" said Ray.

"Exactly. It's the details that make it not just work, but work right. The ridges on the second table, for instance. Running longways. Hold the bales on, no slipping to the left or right. On a perfectly flat field you wouldn't need them."

"But where are you going to find that?" said Al's uncle.

"Exactly. So, the ridges. No extra moving parts,

nothing to break off. They just work."

"So," said Al, "do you think it was an engineer or a farmer who thought of that one?"

"Ha! Who do you think?"

"The first models didn't have the push-off feet, did they?" Al asked. "I remember you had to tilt it up, set the braces and pull forward—"

"And hope for the best," said Johnny.

"And restack it by hand every third load," Al's uncle concluded.

That explains the shoulders on these guys, Betty thought: years of tossing hay bales around. Even with the more reliable machines, she could see that the farm work had toned up Al's upper body.

Great shoulders on this guy.

"Are you guys getting spoiled with all this high-tech equipment now?" she asked with a wink at Al. They all chuckled.

"Every new moving part," proclaimed Johnny, "provides at least two new opportunities for things to go wrong. Even the basic stuff can get you. Like U-joints. Right, Al?"

Everyone but Betty chortled or laughed while Al nodded and grinned at the beer bottle between his feet.

"Especially U-joints."

Betty looked around the group. She'd heard the punchline, but the set-up was apparently somewhere in the past. She raised an eyebrow at Johnny. He winked at her. "This one's for Al to tell," he said. "It's his story."

She turned to Al and raised the same eyebrow. He winked at her. "They're being merciful, letting me tell this one." He cleared his throat and looked up, toward the mountains. "I was seventeen, eighteen at the time. It was haying season. They had me on the mower, where I'd do the least harm. Or so they thought. Do you know what a U-joint is?"

Betty slowly shook her head.

U-joint—the U stands for Universal. When you have a shaft that has to bend while it's turning, there has to be a joint in it. So there is a universal joint at the turning point of the shaft. It's like an elbow or knee joint that swings both ways." Al demonstrated by holding his arms up and putting his fists together with his knuckles interlocked. "One end of the shaft locks onto a connection that sticks out from the back of the tractor's transmission. It's called a power take-off, or PTO, because it takes the power of the tractor and transfers it to another machine."

"Power takeoff sounds like something you'd do with a jet engine."

"Yeah, I know. Now this . . . what was I talking about?"

"Universal joints."

"Right. So, that shaft, from the tractor's PTO to the machine, in this case the hay mower, has a U-joint in it . . ."

"So it can, sort of, bend when you turn corners."

"Right. You keep it lubricated. It's heavy-duty hardware. The thing can outlast the rest of the machine."

"So you're driving the tractor, with the mower. You're seventeen or eighteen years old."

"Half cocky and half terrified. At the time, more cocky. In a quiet sort of way; there was no audience anywhere near. I'm racing along at four miles per hour." Al reached forward to grab an imaginary steering wheel from the air. He hooked his right arm over the back of his chair. "Everything is going fine. The sun's shining. The blades are sharp. The crop is tall and the field is smooth. The tractor is rumbling along the way it should. There's a windrow falling out in a nice, neat line behind the mower." Al rocked on his chair and looked over his shoulder periodically as he spoke. He spoke slowly, leaving a little space between the sentences, until he said, "And suddenly, the mower goes quiet. Another noise replaces it, and it doesn't sound healthy. I turn around and, sure enough, the mower isn't mowing. I hit the clutch and the brakes, and I see the front part of the shaft spinning away on the PTO at 540 revolutions per minute. Half of the U-joint is flopping crazy on the end of it. I throw the PTO lever backward, out of gear. And there's part of the shaft still rolling on the ground. All of this takes about a second. I get off the tractor for a closer look."

"Still cocky?"

"No, I've swung to the other end of the scale. I'm wondering what I did to break the thing. I get down and pick up the part of the shaft that's lying on the ground. I look at it. I pick up a few little pieces of metal still on the ground. They're hot to the touch. The thing just blew apart.

"I gather up the all the loose bits and get back on the tractor. I put the mower into its road position and drive it back to the yard.

"The old guy here," Al pointed at his uncle, "is on the baler. I walk out to the south field to flag him down and he comes in to look at the damage. He shakes his head and gets that bewildered look on his face. He starts taking the thing apart—"

"The rest of the way apart," said Johnny. "You'd had a good start on it."

"True enough. It's a one-man job, so he sends me off to take over on the baler."

Al shifted in his seat, put his left hand back on the steering wheel, and hooked his right elbow over the back of the chair.

"I'm racing along at four miles per hour. Everything is going fine. The sun's shining. The windrows are thick and dry. The field is smooth. The tractor is rumbling along the way it should. There are bales falling out in a nice, neat row behind the baler."

Al paused in his narration and rocked in his chair, looking over his shoulder periodically. After a minute, he said, "And suddenly, the baler goes quiet. Another noise replaces it, and it doesn't sound healthy. I turn around and, sure enough, the baler isn't baling. I hit the clutch and the brakes, and I see the front part of the shaft spinning away on the PTO at 540 revolutions per minute. Half of the U-joint is flopping crazy on the end of it. I throw the PTO lever backward, out of gear. And there's part of the shaft still rolling on the ground. All this takes about a second. I get off the tractor for a closer look.

"I pick up the part of the shaft that's lying on the ground. I look at it. I pick up a few little pieces of metal still on the ground. They're hot to the touch. The thing just blew apart.

"I gather up the all the loose bits and get back on the tractor. I put the baler into its road position and drive it back to the yard. Johnny's come in with the stacker, so they're both at the workbench. They look up to watch me drive in. I hold up half of the broken U-joint. They're both just frozen to the spot, staring at me. I don't even say a word. I shut off the motor. I carry the parts over and set them down on the workbench. We look at them all for a while. Finally, he says to me . . ."

Al turned to his uncle and left the last line of the story for him:

"'So, do you want to give the stacker a try now?'"

◆ ◆ ◆

Betty and Al sat just below the crest of the plateau overlooking the Bow River. They'd walked through the fields and crossed the highway after dinner. After sitting silently for a while, Betty put her hand on Al's knee and said, "I can't believe this, the way you can see all the details so far in the distance. And all the shades and colours of the fields."

"You should see it just after dawn," said Al. "It's the same thing, but with the light penetrating into the west."

"You'll have to wake me up for that."

Al raised both his eyebrows; he'd never been able to do just one the way Betty could.

"Yes, I'll let you do that," Betty continued. "It'll be worth it." It would be worth the disorientation of going to bed earlier than her mind and body preferred. It would be worth the hateful feeling of getting out of bed too early, too. It would be worth it to see this land as Al did.

"I'm not saying I won't bite, but I'd like to see it."

Al put his arm around her. "Maybe I'll be safe from your bite if you wake up to the smell of breakfast cooking."

Johnny stood at his sink, thinking and running water. He was feeling a little off balance. It wasn't the beer—he'd only had one. He may have been affected by the long, hot day running the haystacker. The heat was getting to him more as he got older. Older, he thought. I guess seventy-two is getting there.

Johnny was one of the Old Bachelors of Bearspaw. Every rural community has some, widowers or men who just never married. Being an Old Bachelor is much like holding an elected office—or a holy one, without the prescribed vows. Everyone knows at least one Old Bachelor. An Old Bachelor's kitchen is a place for strict confidences and startling gossip, sometimes in the same sentence.

An Old Bachelor's home—especially his kitchen—is both more public and more private than most family-infested abodes.

Johnny had stayed at the Sutherland place until 8:30. It was always good to eat at a neighbour's. His own repertoire of meals was limited, and as he got older and his stomach got fussier, even more so. He could hardly stand beef anymore. Strange, for a man who always had cattle on his land. He was eating more potatoes and vegetables now. His wiry body was getting even thinner, while so many of his friends were getting heavier.

Young Al and his girlfriend or wife—Johnny wasn't quite sure—were making the meals at the Sutherland place. She worked at a restaurant out in Vancouver, she said. It showed. Fast in the kitchen. Fancy ways of serving up a meal. Some fancy foods, too, but as long as he could recognize something, he didn't mind eating it. She made it taste good, whatever it was.

Johnny turned off the water and stood at his sink for a few moments. His old border collie sat on the lawn, sniffing at odours and notions carried conveniently in on the breeze. Johnny looked around himself. He looked back at the table and realized he had no dirty dishes. This sometimes happened when he ate out.

He always did the dishes late in the day. It put

things in order. Following the routine, he hardly noticed doing it, and the place seemed to take care of itself. He wiped down the clean countertop and drained the sink.

He took off his clothes in the bathroom and shook them out over the tub to get out the dust and grass. The undershirt, socks, and underwear went into a hamper. His shirt and pants were clean enough for another day; these he would hang over the chair in his bedroom.

Johnny rinsed the dust and grass down the drain using the shower head, then put in the plug and started running water for a bath. He put on sweatpants and a T-shirt and went out to feed the dog.

"There you go, Angus," he said. "Nothing fancy, but you seem to like it still." He squatted down and scratched the border collie's ears. "Thirteen years of the same stuff and you never complain. Must be on to something." The Sutherland place was visible down the hill to the southwest. The wind was coming from that direction. He could see the new stacks lined up near the windbreak. Twelve hundred bales today. "Not too bad for an old guy, eh, Angus?"

The tub was a little too full when he came in. He turned off the taps and climbed in. A little too hot, but still okay. He watched the water rise as he settled in, and listened as the excess water trickled down the top vent and into the drainpipes. He washed and rinsed and sat and thought.

A simple thing, that vent. The simple things are always the important parts of any system, however complex. Of course, most complicated machines are made up of the most simple of machines—levers, screws, wheels. A machine can be kept going almost indefinitely by replacing those simple machines and parts within it. Eventually you can replace every part of it and still think of it as the same machine. It's like the joke about the old Swede who passes his axe on to his grandson, saying, "This is the very same axe I brought with me from the Old Country. I've replaced the handle eight times and the head twice, but it's still as good as when I arrived in Canada . . ."

Johnny laughed out loud at the old joke. Old jokes are the best. But it's true, he thought. Even the human body is like that. He'd read somewhere that every cell, from bone marrow to the organs, from muscle tissue to skin, replaces itself at least once every seven years. Johnny rubbed the soap bar over his torso, completely different from the one he was washing in the same tub, say, eight years ago. Looks about the same. Same scar on his left arm. The same pain in his knee before a change in the weather. It was the most reliable forecasting system he knew of for the past thirty years—four complete changes of body.

Today the knee felt pretty good.

• • •

His bedroom was larger than he needed it to be, but it was easy to keep clean. Once a week, on Sunday, he'd strip the bed and vacuum the floor. He always put the clean sheets on in the evening after the mattress had a chance to air out.

He pulled the tools out of their leather pouches on his belt before hanging his pants on the chair. Standing over an enamelled wash basin on his dresser, he opened up his Swiss Army knife and shook it gently to dump any dirt out. He took a Q-tip and cleaned the knife out carefully before putting a drop of oil at each moving joint.

He repeated the process for his six-inch Vice-Grip locking pliers.

Johnny opened up his new Leatherman multitool and looked at it intently as he cleaned it. He had bought it last winter after having looked it over many times. Two parallel arms folded out to become the handles of a set of pliers. Within each arm was a variety of blades, files, and screwdrivers. Johnny found that his hand now sought it before the Swiss Army knife. The Leatherman had proved itself as more than a mere gadget.

He could have bought a cheaper copy of the Leatherman, but Johnny always bought the original brand name of a good tool. The money and the honour were more likely to go to the originator that way. In this case, it was a better tool than any of its imitators.

Johnny had built and varnished a stand for each of the tools he carried on his belt. They were arranged around a small lever and a plaque that read:

Give me a place to stand
and I could move the world.
                    —Archimedes

Directly behind the tools was a cheap plaster bust of a vaguely Greek-looking man with large eyes and a curly beard. When he found the bust at a farm auction years ago, Johnny instantly decided it had to be the ancient physicist Archimedes. He paid a ridiculous price for it and the box of household knick-knacks it was in. Now he seldom looked at the plaque or the bust, except on Sunday afternoons when he did his dusting, but they were always present.

Johnny turned off the two lamps that lit the bust and the tools. He wound his alarm clock and set a couple of Rolaids out on his bedside table.

Johnny was asleep before this sliver of the world had completely turned its back on the sun.

"So, what do you have there?"

Betty turned around to see Herb Sutherland had come into the kitchen. She handed him a bottle and said, "I was thinking you might be able to tell me what I have here."

The older man looked at the fist-sized bottle. It had a strip of soft metal below the rim of the neck.

"This would be an old medicine bottle. Maybe veterinary drugs. It's old, for sure. Where did you get it?"

"I found it poking out of the ground when I was walking in the pasture across the highway. I found these over there as well." There were three other bottles lined up on the counter. The sink was half-full of dirty, soapy water. Betty had been working for some time with a bottle brush, scrubbing them out. "It was the strangest thing. This one was just lying on top of the ground. These others were half-buried, sticking up like they were sprouting. Like plants."

"Frost heave."

"Frost heave?" Betty was clearly confused by the expression, and Sutherland was confused by the fact that Betty was confused. Al had overheard some of the conversation as he came into the kitchen. He laughed at them both.

"She's born and raised in Vancouver, Uncle Herb. They don't have the same experience there with frost setting into the ground." He put down a guitar pick and picked up a squat, round bottle. "So this would have been buried just under the surface at some point. When the ground freezes and thaws, it expands and contracts. You can imagine what that can do to roads in terms of bumps and potholes. Every spring the frost heave squirts up a fresh crop of rocks onto the fields. Grampa always said it was a case of the earth 'calving out.'"

Betty reached into the sink and pulled out a colourless bottle with raised lettering. "And once in a while now it'll bring up a Lambert's Listerine bottle?"

Sutherland picked up another and read the raised letters on the glass. "Watkins. And this other one would be an old whisky bottle."

"Those haven't changed much," said Betty. "Except most of them are plastic now."

"Where exactly did you find these? Across the highway, you said."

Betty nodded. "At the edge of those trees. The poplars."

"On the west side of them?"

Betty had to think for a moment. "The west side. Yes."

Al smiled to himself. He was turning what looked like a Tabasco bottle around in his hands. "I'm always impressed with your waitressing instincts, Betty." He put his arm around her. "If there are empties that need clearing up, you'll find 'em."

Betty suffered the joke in silence. "Okay, so the frost heave makes the bottles pop out of the ground. How did they get there in the first place?"

Sutherland held up a finger as if to say, wait a minute. He went down the hall and returned with a photo album. He set it on the table and opened the plain blue cover. "This is the spot," he said, with his finger on a black-and-white picture. Betty and Al looked at it. "The homestead. Those bottles would have come from the spot where they dumped and buried their garbage. There was no public dump in those days. Every farm had a spot where they would dump the garbage that they couldn't reuse or burn or compost."

Betty sat down to study the photograph. It showed a small, square house with shingle siding. A young man was sitting on a horse to the right. Off to the left, outside of a low fence, were some willow bushes. Beyond the house, the ground dropped away where the slope to the river valley began. In the distance stood the mountains. It took some time for Betty to identify the photo as a picture of the place where she had been taking her early morning walks for the past two weeks. It didn't look right. She glanced through some of the other photographs, occasionally picking out a familiar landmark.

"Trees," she said. "That's what's missing. There are hardly any trees in these pictures. There's plenty of willow, but no poplars. Not like now. They're everywhere now."

"No, the poplars didn't really start taking over until after the war, or about then. World War II, that is." Sutherland leaned over and flipped the pages back to the beginning of the album. "Those first pictures would have been from just before the first war. It was mostly willow scrub then, with the odd spruce."

"What would cause that? Why would it change from the willow to poplar forest?" Betty looked at the pictures again. "All within a generation or two."

"When one thing changes, other things are going

to change, too," said Al. "Bring in a whole lot of cows and get them grazing, it'll change things. They'll eat certain plants, leave others alone. It gives some plants a chance to get going where they couldn't compete before."

"It could be that the buffalo were prone to chew down saplings that the cattle aren't interested in, too," said Sutherland.

Betty was looking out the window. "It's weird. I look at the land, at the pasture land that's never been cultivated, and I think it seems so wild and so old. I guess I think of wilderness as being permanent. But it changes. Slowly, maybe, but always changing." She put a hand against the wood of the window frame. "Like any other living thing." She shrugged off a shiver and turned. "Is there anything left of the house in that picture?"

"Oh, that old shack is long gone now," said Sutherland.

"The foundation is still there, isn't it?" said Al.

"Oh, sure it is. Just beyond those trees."

"So it's easy to find," said Betty. She was up and pouring coffee in the Thermos and putting some of Al's muffins into a canvas shoulder bag. She paused for a moment. "It rained last night, so you guys aren't making any hay today, right?" Sutherland nodded. "So what do you say we all go." It wasn't a question, nor was it an order. Al went to find their camera.

Sutherland stood at the table with the pictures. Without looking up, he said, "Sure, let's do that."

• • •

Sutherland hesitated beside his truck. Al and Betty had walked past it and were still walking. "I guess a walk wouldn't hurt me any," he muttered as he put away his key.

As they walked, they talked. Betty was full of questions; Sutherland was full of information. She wanted to know which buildings were built when, and what they were for. Sutherland told her about the whole idea of homesteading. He described how the old house grew room by added-on room as the family had grown, baby by baby.

Betty looked at Sutherland's sun-mottled, wrinkled face. He had been one of those babies; as a child he had slept in one of those lean-to additions. She looked up at Al's face, with the same chin and nose as his uncle. Returning to the farm had obviously been good for Al. He was simply more himself. She'd been soaking up this place, watching and listening to the people and their stories, seeing Al work on farm machinery, of all things, and listening to him play his instruments in the evening. Only with Al did Betty think of the bass guitar as a solo instrument.

Now she was seeing that there was more history to this man of hers than she'd realized.

They turned onto the main road and headed south toward the 1A highway. On their left was a development, Cameron Estates, named for the family whose farm had been bulldozed to make room for, as Sutherland put it, "a bunch of three-acre houses on four-acre lots." Betty remembered Al telling her about the reaction of one old-timer when he saw the first of those mansions being built: Why would anybody build a shopping centre out here? The old man couldn't imagine anything that big being a private dwelling.

Betty turned her attention back to the road. She looked ahead to the 1A and asked, "When did they put the highway in? It cuts right through the middle of your land."

"Actually, the road was there from before. It was the main route from Calgary to Cochrane and Morley. It was originally called the Morley Trail. It was just a path to start with. For horses and carts. Or people on foot. In fact, the Indians used it before the railway or the homesteaders came."

"That goes back a ways."

"Hundreds of years, probably."

"Maybe thousands," added Al.

Betty let this sink in as she watched a Safeway truck roll westbound along the highway. Older than the Roman highways in England, she thought to herself. After a few moments, she said aloud, "Is there anything left of it now? I mean, the original trail."

"Oh, there's no sign of it anymore," said Sutherland. "It's mostly under all that earth and asphalt, or grown over."

"There were teepee rings, though," said Al. "I remember Mom talking about them."

"Teepee rings?" asked Betty.

"Yeah, teepee rings. You know, the rocks that were used to weigh down the bottom edges of the teepees. They would be left in place so they wouldn't have to gather and arrange the stones every time they came back to set up camp."

"The things you miss when you grow up in Vancouver. So, where were they?" asked Betty.

"South of the highway," said Sutherland. "Just back from the edge of the escarpment. Near the old homestead, in fact."

"Are they still there? Can we find them?"

"They should be there still," said Sutherland. "It's

not much to look at. Just some small boulders set out in circles. We should be able to find them."

♦ ♦ ♦

As they walked, they could see a couple approaching from the road into Cameron Estates. The woman appeared to be holding a curved stick ahead of her. As they drew closer, a small grey dog appeared at her feet. The stick was actually a leash. The man stopped and waved, then turned and said something to the woman. She nodded assent to whatever he had said. They stood and waited until Sutherland, Al, and Betty reached them. The dog was lying down at their feet. It was either a mutt or an exotic purebred. The couple were smiling as if they were waiting for a camera to flash. They wore outfits that, while not identical, seemed to have been chosen very carefully to match. Their walking shoes were identical. The man said, "Good afternoon, Mr. Sutherland." His arm was coming forward to shake hands, but Sutherland had his hands in his pockets and was rocking from his toes to his heels. He wore a half-grin on his face and raised his eyebrows in an expression approaching quizzical.

This is interesting, thought Al. Uncle Herb is putting on his yokel act.

The man let his hand fall a moment before it would have been obvious and embarrassing. "We've met a time or two. The name's Chapel, Charles Chapel. This is my wife, Camilla."

"You're kid—" began Betty, then she coughed to cut herself off. "Pardon me."

"I remember you," said Sutherland. "This is my nephew, Al, and his, er . . ."

Betty saved Sutherland from having to find a word almost equivalent to *wife*; she reached out to shake hands. "Hi, I'm Betty." Camilla shook her hand and smiled with relief.

"I'm glad we ran into you," said Charles. "We've been wanting to talk to you about something."

"Is that so."

"Indeed." Charles and Camilla looked at each other and, in unison, gave a short, decisive nod. "Yes, we have. First, we want you to know how much we enjoy living out here. It's such beautiful country. Every day we look out the window and just take it all in." Camilla nodded. Throughout her husband's speech, she would give a single nod, almost a bow, at strategic moments.

"We've been here for four and a half years. Haven't gotten tired of it, not in the least. How could we? How could we get tired of this view?" He gestured toward the mountains, the sweep of his arm including the Sutherland farm. "We spent most of my working years living in the city, but we always wanted a country place. Now we have it. I was a dentist, you see, but I'm retired now. I sold the practice to one of my younger partners. I can manage my investments from home with my computer. The Internet, you know. Hardly need the city anymore." As he spoke, Charles Chapel shifted his attention and his gaze between Sutherland, Betty, and Al like a seasoned public speaker. It struck Al that the man *sounded* like a seasoned public speaker, everything he said ringing with preparation and rehearsal. "In fact, my office is up on the third floor, with the window on this side. There, the second house back from the road." He pointed past a construction site with a couple of carpenters installing floor joists on a new foundation. His house was a five-thousand-square-foot structure, an uneasy synthesis of at least three distinct and uncooperative architectural styles. "I can look up from my computer and look out on all this. Beautiful. Now, Mr. Sutherland," he said, turning to focus his attention on the old farmer while speaking in a tone that was meant to address a larger audience, "I'm sure that you know that your land is worth a lot of money. Any number of developers would jump at the chance to buy you out. There's a lot of money to be made by subdividing it." Charles indulged in a very obvious pause. "We want you to know that, whatever offer you get from a developer, we'll match it. Not to develop it, mind you—"

Much to Charles' surprise, Camilla interrupted him: "We wouldn't develop it. We love it too much. It's so lovely. We'd happily buy it just to keep it as it is. You see, we don't want a whole lot of houses going up right across the road from us."

"Oh, I can understand that, all right," said Sutherland. Betty saw the glimmer of an ironic smile on his face.

"We're serious about this," said Charles. "Absolutely serious. Here's our number." He held out a glossy business card. This time Sutherland could see no way to get away with keeping his hands in his pockets. He accepted the card, looked at it and nodded, and tucked it into his shirt pocket.

"I'll keep that in mind."

Charles nodded; Camilla looked at him with a satisfied smile. "Good," she said. "We should keep moving, Charles. Our little friend is getting restless." She tugged at the leash to wake up the tiny dog. She smiled again and they went on their way.

Betty watched them go. That was Camilla's idea,

she thought to herself. Offering to buy the land. He did the talking, but she's the one who thought it through.

Sutherland chuckled and relaxed out of his yokel persona. He shook his head and started to walk again. "At least they didn't use the word *quaint*," he said. "I hate it when people call a farm quaint. But I'll still take their offer with more than a grain of salt. I have to say, it's original. Nobody's made me that kind of offer before." They walked on for a few minutes in silence. Sutherland absently kicked a Budweiser can from the shoulder of the road into the ditch. "Of course, even if they did buy it, there's nothing to stop them from changing their minds and subdividing it eventually."

"Actually, there is," said Al. "In fact, there are a couple of ways to do it. You can have a conservancy easement put on your land when you sell it or hand it down as an inheritance. I'm not sure exactly how it works, but it is legally binding. Or you can put it into a land trust. The Glasers did that a few years ago."

"Oh, that's right. I heard something about that," said Sutherland.

Al explained to Betty that the Glasers were an old farming family from a few miles northwest of the Sutherland place. "It made the news, even in Vancouver. I think they were the first farmers in Alberta to do it."

"Hmm," said Sutherland. He had a habit of saying *hmm* when he was dismissing an idea as irrelevant, or when storing the information away for later use. Either way, Al knew it was time to drop the topic.

• • •

As they waited for the highway traffic to pass, Betty tried to tune out the noise and the rush of air to imagine the same place without vehicles, without houses, without asphalt. Without poplars, without fences, without domestic crops growing in the soil. She tried to picture only prairie grasses and willow, with a path a little wider than a game trail snaking along the land. She could do it; for a moment, when she closed her eyes, she could see it that way.

She opened her eyes and saw that the road was clear. They started across.

As they passed onto the eastbound lanes, Betty saw something move in the median. She looked and caught sight of a coyote lying in the grass. He tilted his head and opened his mouth in a grin. At least, she thought it was a grin. She grinned back. The coyote didn't seem at all concerned with their proximity. She looked up and touched Al on the arm. He turned to her and she pointed, but when she looked, the coyote was gone. She stopped, then shook her head as if to say, never mind.

Betty led the way to the spot where she'd found the bottles. They walked in through the poplars. Al almost tripped on an old bucket, half-buried in the ground. • 77 • They carried on, with Sutherland now leading the way. They passed between two spruce trees, arranged almost as a gateway out of the forest. Betty ran her hand along the smooth bark of the tree. She had to duck to keep her head below the lowest branches. She noticed that the bark above the lowest branches was rough. She pointed this out. Al explained that the cows would eat spruce boughs for the needles, and they liked to rub themselves on the bark, especially in the spring, to rub off their winter coats. Betty raised an eyebrow at him.

"No, really. In fact, every January we would take all the decorations off the Christmas tree and toss it out in the pasture. The cows go nuts over the stuff. It must have some minerals in it that they can't get any other way." She ran her hand over the tree trunk again and looked closely at it. As polished and smooth as it was, it still held some coarse, off-white hairs from what could only be a cow.

Betty turned around and followed Sutherland over to a spot away from the trees. He was looking down at something. At first she thought it was a pile of rocks. As she came closer, she realized that it was the foundation of the old farmhouse. The concrete was coarse, with large stones mingled with smaller gravel in the mix. The centre had collapsed and the sides had broken apart as they leaned and toppled inward. It looked like an open mouth with teeth broken beyond any hope of orthodontic remedy. She walked around it, looking into it. Soil had built up within the centre of the hole, and a spindly wild rose bush had taken root there.

Al counted his long paces along the dimensions of it. "It's a bit smaller than our apartment," he told her. "Of course that doesn't account for the outhouse."

"How many people lived in this house?"

Sutherland answered, "Our folks lived here until their third child came along. That was Al's father. By then, Dad had built the new place over where I live now. It was more sheltered from the wind than here, and this house was a bit drafty, or so I'm told."

"So that picture was taken from . . ." Betty began.

"Over there, from the northeast," said Sutherland.

Al walked over to the vantage point and took a few pictures. Betty was sitting on one of the broken slabs and Sutherland stood off to the right, looking east. He could see the towers of downtown Calgary from there. Weeks later, Al would look at that photograph and try to read the expression on his uncle's face.

Sutherland shrugged. He said, "You can imagine why the Indians would choose this spot for a camp. It's handy to the trail. There's water from the spring down there in the coulee. You can see for miles, looking for game or watching out for enemies."

Yes, thought Betty in the silence. I can imagine it.

"Well," said Sutherland. "Do you want to find those teepee rings now?"

◆ ◆ ◆

The three of them walked slowly toward the edge of the escarpment, scanning the ground as they went. Al stopped to look at a rock. Betty and Sutherland joined him and fanned out from that point. They found other rocks, but scattered in zigzag patterns rather than rings. No amount of imagination could force the stones, as they lay, into a circle. They continued on, away from the homestead site. Again they found promising rocks; again, no real pattern could be read in their placement.

Betty asked Al for the camera. She wasn't finding teepee rings, but she was seeing things entirely new to her. The lichen on these Alberta rocks crawled with subtle yet vivid colours. She took close-up shots. She also stooped to examine the plants. She took some pictures of them, with little hope of doing them justice. She tried to keep track of the different species of plants, at first giving them the names of friends—Louise and Carol and Sarah—then losing track and resorting to simply counting. All the time, she continued to look for rocks in circles.

They reached the edge of the land where it dropped off sharply into a coulee. No teepee rings had been found. Sutherland looked around himself in the manner of someone in a hurry looking for a set of car keys. Without saying a word, he turned and hurried back to the concrete slabs. Al and Betty caught up to him. He was walking in a slow circle around the foundation, saying, "I remember them. They were near the old house. I just don't remember exactly where." He wouldn't look up to meet their eyes, and Al and Betty could tell that he wasn't expecting a reply. They could see the tension in his face. Sutherland led them in a slow spiral, growing out from their starting point. Again they walked and searched for any group of rocks forming a circle or even a vague arc.

They wound up among the youngest poplars that grew on the edge of the copse. Sutherland said, "It's possible that the trees have grown up among them.

These trees right here would all be less than fifteen or twenty years old. That's nothing in the big picture." The grass was taller in among the trees. Sutherland broke a branch off of an older tree and brought it back to sweep the grass aside. He pushed past or over the young trees, sometimes stopping at a rock to search for a second or third stone. Al and Betty could see that the process was next to hopeless, but they couldn't find a gentle way to say it. Sutherland broke through the trees and his search became erratic. "They were here. Somewhere. They were here." Finally he stopped walking. He was sweating and breathing heavily. He turned back and forth in tight semicircles, muttering, "Maybe they've been kicked around by the cows. Maybe some kids just rolled them off into the coulee. Maybe—they might be deeper in the trees."

His hands twitched at his sides. Betty had never seen the old man agitated like this. She could tell from Al's face that he hadn't either. An instinct or an intuition, sharpened by years of waiting tables, led her to pull the Thermos and mugs out of the canvas bag. She set the mugs down on a level piece of ground and filled them with coffee. She pulled out a muffin and took it with a coffee over to Sutherland. He accepted them automatically. Now, he had something to do with his hands. Now, he had something in his mouth to crowd out the ineffectual words. And so did Betty and so did Al.

◆ ◆ ◆

The walk home was almost silent, but not as awkward as it might have been. Sutherland had relaxed while eating his second muffin. At one point, the old farmer stopped chewing and said, "Hmm." He seemed to have found his equilibrium in that moment. Some thought had occurred to him, or some decision had been made. No more was said about it.

◆ ◆ ◆

Betty and Al went into town for dinner that night. Betty had an agenda. She did most of the talking. There was a question she needed the answer to.

"What happened to your uncle out there today? Why did he freak out like that?"

"Something really got to him."

"No kidding. It was like he was getting all obsessive-compulsive about those teepee rings."

"No. For it to be obsessive-compulsive behaviour, I think it has to be part of a larger pattern, or an ongoing thing."

"That's what made it so weird. It wasn't part of a pattern for him. It wasn't like him. So what was it?"

"Let's look at what happened."

"Okay. The last thing that happened, the thing that seemed to trigger his freak-out, was the teepee rings. Not finding them. And that's weird, because it didn't seem so important to him when we started out. We weren't even talking about them until we were halfway down the road."

"So what were we talking about?"

Betty thought about this for a while.

"Change," she said. "We were talking about things changing. Things changing in big ways, but gradually, so you don't notice the fact that they're changing."

"'Don't it always seem to go,'" quoted Al, "'That you don't know what you got . . .'"

Betty hummed the rest of the line.

"If the teepee rings can disappear and be forgotten," she said, "what's to say anything else won't be swallowed up by the earth?" She rolled her empty beer bottle back and forth between her hands. She didn't have an answer to her question.

◆ ◆ ◆

A few days later, Betty was cleaning more bottles. After

she found the first batch, she started finding more. They seemed to pop out of the ground in answer to her footsteps. She also found some machine parts and an old hunting knife with a handle carved out of deer antler. As far as she could tell, none of it was simply junk. Most of it was, at least, old. After cleaning it up, each item was given a spot on the windowsill in Betty and Al's room. Some of the items took a fair bit of cleaning. She left the last few bottles soaking in bleach and water in a bucket outside and followed the sound of Al's guitar into the basement.

Al was sitting on a chair with a dozen music books open on the table in front of him. He was playing a country swing tune that was more than halfway to jazz. Betty snuck a peek at the book he was playing from. She was surprised. Al laughed at her. "You're surprised?"

"Wilf Carter?"

"You bet. The man could swing. Think of it as Lyle Lovett without quite so much irony."

"Keep playing."

Al played. Betty picked up some of the songbooks and flipped through them. Once in a while her eyebrows would pop up. "Something surprising in there?" asked Al.

"There's some pretty gruesome stuff in here. It's not what I expect in old-time country music."

"Before punk or gangster rap, there were outlaw tunes. I think they were necessary, to balance out the more sentimental stuff." Al flipped over a few pages and started on another song. Betty lay back on the couch and listened. She watched her thoughts drift by, bobbing in the music. After a while, Al found some tricky bit that required a fair bit of repetition and involved more mistakes. Betty's thoughts started to sink. She went back upstairs.

The phone was ringing when she came into the kitchen. She rushed into the office and picked it up half a ring too late. As she hung up the phone, she saw a piece of paper on the floor. She picked it up to return it to the desk. She turned it over to see if it was significant or just a piece of litter. In Sutherland's handwriting were written the words, "conservancy ease." and "land trust." She set it down on the desk beside the Rolodex. The Rolodex was flipped open to a card that read, "G. Parry, lawyer."

"Hmm," she said to herself. "Hmm."

Betty had never believed she could be a morning person.

Her first morning walk with Al had been easier than she feared. The reason was simple enough. In July, you had to get up before five to beat the sunrise. That was far earlier than she had ever thought morning to occur, so she was in fact getting up in the middle of the night. That proved easier than getting up at a more typical "morning" hour of, say, eight o'clock.

Betty rolled out of bed and into a pair of sweatpants and a sweater. She couldn't remember tying on her boots, but there they were on her feet as they walked down the driveway. Al was carrying a canvas bag with muffins, a Thermos of coffee, and mugs.

Her boots fascinated her for a few minutes, appearing and disappearing beneath her remarkably quickly. She looked up and looked around her. She let her head bob with the rhythm of her steps. Our steps, she said to herself. If you're actually walking with someone, your steps wind up in unison. One rhythm, at the same tempo.

She looked around herself, at Al and at the fences by the road, at the power poles. She looked at the windrows of hay in the field beside them and the quiet tractor waiting in the field. She looked at a hawk on a fence post, who looked back. There was no breeze, but she could feel the air on her skin and in her hair.

Al and Betty crossed the highway after a lone early commuter passed by, and Betty was amazed at how wide the highway was. It never felt that way from the inside of a car.

They sat down on the edge of the hill and ate their muffins and warmed their hands on the coffee mugs as the sunlight turned the mountains from a bad set of lower teeth into a visible laugh. From that morning on, Betty would always associate the taste of raisins and bran with the early light hitting the Rockies.

She found herself waking up in the darkness—not every day, but often—with time to make a batch of muffins and a pot of coffee before daybreak. Sometimes she'd nudge Al out of bed for a walk. Sometimes she'd just go by herself. At first she'd count power poles to pass the time. After a few solitary walks, she stopped counting, no longer feeling time as needing to be passed.

One morning she saw the silhouette of a neighbour walk onto the hillside.

Several mornings later, Betty walked over to the fenceline and greeted the woman, thinking, This must be Annie. Annie already knew who Betty was. They introduced themselves anyway. Betty crossed through the fence at Annie's invitation and the two of them sat down on the crest of the escarpment. Betty poured a coffee for herself. Annie was already cradling a full mug.

The sun did its trick with the mountains as they watched.

"I never get tired of this," said Annie.

"I'm sure you don't."

"Some things I do get tired of. Like scrubbing floors. Like shovelling snow. Like using the Rototiller. Like gathering up the sections of the newspaper off the carpet. Or writing letters to the editor—they never publish them anymore! Or cleaning out the cat litter . . ." The litany was a long one. Betty smiled discreetly on one side of her face and nodded to dissipate the laughter rising from her chest.

When Annie paused, Betty took a breath and said, "I know what you mean." Annie looked at Betty with a serious expression, than nodded as if something had been confirmed for her. She smiled and looked back to the river valley.

"On the other hand . . ." she said.

"Yes. On the other hand."

Betty shuffled around to take her weight off of a pebble. She opened the Thermos and topped up her mug and Annie's as well.

"Thank you," said Annie with a touch of formality that struck Betty as being appropriate to the setting. "You're Al's wife, or girlfriend . . . ?"

"Yes." Betty saw no need to clarify the point. "We've been together for six years," she said.

"I've seen you walking with him some mornings. You move well together."

Betty raised an eyebrow.

"You can tell a lot about a man by watching him move. Especially when he's doing something he loves. That's how I fell in love with James. Watching him ride. Even on a tired old pony, he can ride like an old waltz."

The turn of phrase startled Betty. She had no reply, but Annie didn't seem to expect one.

◆ ◆ ◆

Six years ago, Betty was serving drinks in a bar with a

front door in East Vancouver and a parking lot in Burnaby. She was twenty-five and plenty old enough to be jaded about bars, bar patrons, and bar bands. She'd sing along with the music while waiting tables, if she could stand the music. This was read as enthusiasm and translated into tips.

She saw Al for the first time on a Wednesday night—Wings Night, with country music. The first thing she noticed about him that night was his beer intake: a glass of draft after the first set and a mug at the end of the night. The only thing remarkable about that was how it compared to the rest of the band. They measured their beer by the jug rather than by the glass or mug. While they were still drinking after closing, Al was packing up the gear. This was how she noticed the second thing about him—his shoulders. Betty moved a few tables out of his way to clear a path to the side door and the van. He smiled at her over the amp he was carrying. His smile was the third thing she noticed.

That band played at the bar a week later. Over the next six months she saw Al play eight times in three different bands. The beer, the shoulders, and the smile; solid bass playing in country, pop, and heavy metal. Every Tuesday night was "Metal Mania." Al was filling in while this band was looking for a permanent bass player. The concept of permanence hardly fit with that bunch. Betty wore discreet earplugs on Tuesday nights and learned to read lips to take orders. It's hard to misinterpret the words *beer* or *draft*.

She was surprised to see Al in a heavy metal band. He caught her puzzled expression and gave her an embarrassed grin. He shrugged those shoulders in his black sleeveless T-shirt. She smiled back and held up her fist in a heavy metal salute that made him laugh. It was their most intimate exchange up to that time, and it occurred across a crowd of beer-chugging rebels in band-logo T-shirts and denim or leather jackets.

She talked to him for the first time a few weeks later when he was playing for a different country-rock band. It was a two-night stand and Al hung around after closing, trying out a few things with the guitar player while the staff cleaned up. Betty was running a mop across the floor in front of the stage and joked, "Do you take requests?"

Al laughed. "We take 'em, but what we do with them is our business. What do you want to hear?"

"Play something you really love, something that you never get to play."

Al looked at Betty for a moment before putting down his bass and picking up an acoustic guitar. He played a long instrumental piece that took an old melody from simple interpretation, through bluegrass and blues incarnations, and back again. Betty watched Al's fingers, the way he bent over the guitar. She watched as one foot, then the other, beat out the tempo as steady as a metronome. The thought occurred to her that Al was more crucial to some of his bands than the drummers for establishing and maintaining the metre. She watched his shoulders rise and fall as he bent his head to watch his left hand or to listen to the body of the guitar. He slowed the tempo and switched to 3/4 time.

He rode that old waltz like a well-broke horse.

She could hear him playing as she sat in silence with Annie. She smiled at the older woman. Annie smiled back and they both nodded.

The sound of a tractor whispered to them from the direction of the Sutherland farm. It was a dry morning and someone was getting an early start. Betty stood up and looked back to see the International tractor pulling the hay mower. "That would be Al," she said. "They have him on the mower."

Annie was looking toward Al very intently, smiling and nodding, and Betty quietly hummed a slow, old waltz.

Weather forecasts cannot be trusted. The summer had already had too many surprise rain-showers. There hadn't been enough precipitation to make it an unusually wet season, but, as in comedy and music, timing is everything for a hay harvest. More than a week had been lost to sporadic rain. Just as the mown crop in the field south of the highway was dry enough to bale, another pile of clouds would trip over the mountains and squeeze themselves out over the foothills.

Now, after two days of solid blue skies, the machines were rolling over the fields, eating hay like a biblical plague of locusts. They'd keep going while the sun shone, so long as they weren't held up by a break-down. This was unlikely—the delay caused by the rain had provided the time for maintenance and repairs. Normally, in mid-harvest, the machines are maintained and repaired to the minimum standard of operation in order to maximize the time spent in the fields. With the extra time, Sutherland and Johnny worked off their restlessness by restoring the mower, baler, and stacker to their pre-season splendour. Everything was working now as it would in a dealer's demonstration video. All the machines were south of the highway. Al was cutting the second of two large fields while his uncle was baling and Johnny was stacking in the first field.

Al had started early. By the time the dew had evaporated enough for the baler to start, Al had been mowing for almost three hours. With no radio, he had only his own thoughts for entertainment. Operating the machine occupied some of his attention, but most of his mind was free to follow its own initiatives. After a few hours, the experience is much like meditation. A good jam session with good musicians can take you to a similar mental place, or state, or province. Al had tried to describe the experience to Betty more than once.

"You never know what your mind will come up with," he explained. "At its best, you'll find yourself in a state of hyperassociation." Betty raised an eyebrow. "It's a word I thought up on the tractor. It's the opposite of disassociation, but just as disorienting. Hyperassociation is the state where you start seeing the way things—objects, ideas, memories, sensations—are connected. Hyperassociation is the state of mind where poetry originates.

"On the other hand, your mind can formulate things that may be best left unthought. Like one day a couple of weeks ago. After six hours of mowing hay I found myself singing the theme song from *The Beverly Hillbillies* to the tune of Steve Earle's "Copperhead Road.""

Betty frowned and hummed a few bars.

"It works, doesn't it," said Al. "Kinda disturbing, I know. Sorry."

"It even makes a kind of sense . . ."

"You probably don't want that running around in your head. Here, this might help," said Al, as he slipped a Santana disc into the CD player.

This was one of those rare days when everything worked well and consistently. Al had to remind himself to stop for lunch; it felt wrong to shut down a machine that was working so well, even for half an hour. His uncle had started later and didn't stop till after two o'clock. Johnny had started an hour after Sutherland and didn't stop at all until suppertime. He was putting up three loads per hour, each load containing ninety-nine bales. By the time they stopped for supper, he was having to wait for the baler to get ahead of him.

They worked late to take advantage of the weather,

and to make up for the week of delays. Supper was at 7:30. During the slow days, Al and Betty had made a flotilla of casseroles in anticipation of the blitz. Tonight was a macaroni and three cheese concoction with ham and vegetables. It was familiar enough for Sutherland to recognize it as food, but still interesting enough to bother cooking. Everyone ate a serving suitable for a teenage boy, except for Johnny. He took a small portion and left almost half of it.

* * *

The next day went as well or better. They worked until eight o'clock. In two days they had put up over three thousand bales of hay.

They ate another enormous casserole for supper. This time, even Sutherland noticed that Johnny ate next to nothing. "You might as well take it easy tomorrow morning, Johnny," he said. "I'll need some time to get ahead of you anyway to get some bales on the ground."

"We'll see, we'll see," said Johnny. "I think I'll make an early night of it, anyway. Good night."

Johnny did make an early night of it. He tried to put his feeling of weakness and exhaustion out of his mind. Might be stomach flu. Never used to get sick.

Never used to feel old. He didn't look in the mirror as he washed his face; he knew how pale he looked.

Sutherland made an early night of it as well. He insisted on doing the dishes. With Al and Betty around for the summer, he'd hardly had to cook a meal for weeks. It was a relief and a luxury, but the old bachelor needed to lay claim to some of his accustomed territory. With the kitchen clean, he sat down to read the stale headlines of the day's newspaper. His mind wandered to his hay crop. The last two days' stacks would require four tarps. Al and Betty had repaired and tied strings onto six tarps in the past week, so he just had to remember to put four of them into the truck in the morning to take over to the field. That was his last thought as he went to bed with an unconscious sense of satisfaction for the last two days' work, and for the life he had never regretted.

Al and Betty sat on the deck on the west side of the house with a few bottles of Big Rock Warthog Ale. Betty read a thick technothriller while Al played his six-string. Sometimes he just doodled around, but tonight he was playing complete songs. Betty looked up from her book. Al's face was tanned from around the eyes and down, below the shade of his ball cap; his arms were tanned from the line of his T-shirt to his gloves. He never looked like this in Vancouver. He also did more doodling on his guitar in Vancouver, except when he was playing a gig. She realized that he played coherent pieces more often since she had joined him on the farm. Al finished what he was playing and reached for his beer. Betty smiled at him and he raised his drink to her. He gave her a look that was half puppy dog and half wicked grin, then slid a run down the low E string into the beginning of a blues number.

The rhythm rocked Betty's head back. She rolled her shoulders as the music ran down into her. She shifted her legs and ignored her book for a while.

Somewhere in the left hemisphere of Al's brain, thoughts about the rural history of the blues were stumbling over the details of the operation of a Case-International Harvester tractor. He played a long improvisation on a 12-bar-blues rendition of "Amazing Grace." He knew it well enough that he could let his fingers do all the thinking and talking. The melody is stretched out from its traditional 3/4 time to fit into a 4/4 rhythm. It is a song that is stuck in the consciousness of almost everybody, a song of repentance and relief written by a guilt-ridden slave-ship captain who borrowed the melody from a smoky tavern drinking song—a song for both the sinner and the saint. It is one of those perfectly crafted songs that seems to simply exist. Al couldn't remember when he had first heard the song. At church, maybe, or on television. He was sure that he'd heard it at every funeral he'd ever been to.

It was like those other things that are stuck in your earliest memories, the things that combine with your genes to make you what you are: memories for Al of his childhood on the farm—the smell of new hay, the shallow scratches in the skin from the bales, heat radiating from the sun and from the tractor engines. There is a sense of time based on the cycle of seasons and harvests, rather than mere days or weeks. There was never a question of the rightness, the validity of the work or the life of farming. It was simply there, always. It was a long ways from playing the same forty classic rock songs in third-rate bars for months on end. Strange, he thought, moving as he had from the one life to the other.

"Amazing Grace, how sweet the sound . . ." Al sung the verse silently as he played.

When he finished playing, Al put his guitar back in its case and opened another beer. Betty propped a foot on his now-vacant knee.

When they went to bed, Al was tired, but not too tired to make love.

◆ ◆ ◆

Morning came, bright and warm. Al and Betty went

with Sutherland immediately after breakfast to tarp the stacks. There was no wind, and it wasn't too hot. The job is much more difficult with even a slight breeze to lift a tarp like a sail. It took less than an hour and a half to get the tarps on and tacked down. Al and Betty stayed to tighten and double-check every string while Sutherland returned to the air-conditioned tractor to start baling. Al and Betty drove the pickup truck over to the mower and greased and oiled it. They shared a long, slow kiss while the tractor warmed up, then Betty started to walk home as Al opened the throttle and started up the mower. Betty waved to Johnny as he drove into the field.

The day heated up quickly. The impatience from two days before was gone, replaced by a satisfying sense of momentum. The grass was drying almost as fast as it was being cut, the baler pumped out the bales with nonchalant confidence, and the stacks seemed to build themselves.

The shadows crawled under the tractors, then slowly out again toward the east.

Al was just starting to think about supper when one discordant note sounded in his mind. Everything had been going so smoothly. It took him a minute of scanning the fields to see what wasn't right. The stacker was stopped, and it had been for a few minutes. It's normal to have to stop to adjust things from time to time, or to have a drink or take a leak. This was somehow different. Al finished off a corner and pushed a lever to raise the mower. He shut off the power to the machine and geared up and drove toward the stacker.

Al and his uncle got to the stacker at the same time. The tractor's engine was running at a slow idle. The machine had been shut off. An untidy pile of bales lay on the table of the machine. Among them was Johnny. He lay face down and twisted over the forward edge of the table. His body was curled in a crescent around his stomach, which was impaled on a metal spike. An identical spike on the far corner of the table was showing. For some reason or another, Johnny had had to stop and rearrange the bales on the fifth layer, the tie layer, where the bales are laid in a pattern to create right angles against the other layers, which stabilizes the whole load. Somehow he had slipped or a bale rolled under his feet and he came down hard on exactly the wrong spot.

Sutherland drove his truck at highway speeds across the field to use a neighbour's phone. Al stayed behind to gently staunch the wound with his T-shirt. He crawled under the machine to unbolt the spike. Johnny still had a faint pulse, but that was the only discernable movement in his body. Sutherland returned and helped Al turn Johnny around to a better position. They stayed with him without talking until an ambulance arrived, bumping over the field with its lights flashing.

Sutherland rode in the ambulance with Johnny. Al was left, standing shirtless and covered in drying blood. He watched the ambulance crawl carefully over the field and climb onto the highway. The siren came on. Al watched until the flashing lights disappeared. Then he went from tractor to tractor, shutting off the engines.

• • •

The funeral happened three days later.

Johnny, or at least parts of his body, lived through the trip to the hospital, and for a couple of hours more. The doctor who watched the old man die had found the spike was embedded in a tumour the size of a grapefruit. A little more probing revealed cancer spreading like suburbs throughout Johnny's abdomen.

Johnny looked good in the casket, wearing his one suit. The funeral parlour was half full with living farmers, looking less comfortable in their suits and ties. Even the city relatives didn't seem comfortable in their clothes, although many of them wore ties every day. Al looked around and thought, No one ever looks comfortable in a funeral parlour, whatever they are wearing.

Al saw a lot of familiar faces in the room. Some he had to imagine with less weight or more hair before he could recall names. Johnny's nieces and nephews were easy to identify, especially as they dominated the family rows near the front. In fact, the faces looked less and less familiar as Al scanned the crowd from the front rows to the back. The back four rows were occupied mostly by people of Johnny's age, in their seventies. There was one exception, a sixteen-year-old boy with both wrists in plaster casts. He was probably the least comfortable of the lot.

Johnny's younger brother, his closest relative, had seen to the arrangements. It was a very conventional funeral; the minister had drawn up a simple, straightforward service, and the family agreed with it entirely. Every element was familiar, and thus comforting. The hymns were ingrained in the rural, protestant mind: A Mighty Fortress Is Our God; Oh The Deep Deep Love of Jesus; Amazing Grace.

When the officiating minister, a United Church pastor, stood up to speak, he didn't even clear his throat. Al had to reconsider his earlier thought; here was one person who looked comfortable in a funeral parlour. Reverend Brian Laidlaw had a warm, round smile and deeply sad eyes. He began speaking in a voice so relaxed that it didn't feel at first like a carefully prepared homily.

"Funerals," he said, "are more for the living than for the dead. Today we offer you the chance to give a voice to your grief and sense of loss, even if that voice must use borrowed words. We turn to hymns to sing together, with words that make more sense than our own thoughts and feelings. We listen to passages of scripture to hear wisdom and compassion passed down to us through the history of the Faith. I know enough of you that I can't make do with a standard-issue sermon. And, although he was more regular in tithing than attending church, I did know Johnny enough to feel qualified to speak today.

"Sometimes when I open my Bible, which of course is part of my job, I ask myself, how will I see this person or that situation described here. There is, of course, the passage in the Psalms that says, 'He owns the cattle on a thousand hills,' but around here I believe that refers to Mr. Harvey." The mourners laughed quietly at the familiar joke. "But we can find passages that will ring true as we remember Johnny." He flipped to a bookmarked page, but recited without looking down at the words: "'Consider the lilies how they grow: they toil not, they spin not; and yet I say unto you, that Solomon in all his glory was not arrayed like one of these. If then God so clothe the grass . . .'"

Al's mind divided, half of it following the preacher, the other following its own paths. He remembered as a teenager with his father, stopping in on Johnny to borrow or return some tool. Johnny was wearing a wild crocus in a buttonhole. When Al noticed it, Johnny quoted the same verses as the preacher was now reciting. "You've got to admire a flower like this," said Johnny. "The first one to show its face in the springtime. They'll sprout up even when there's still snow on the ground. For a flower, that takes guts. Of course, they come prepared, see, with a fur coat." Al recalled Johnny's uneven grin. "Preparation is a great substitute for courage."

Al looked at the general-purpose bouquets of flowers flanking the coffin. The minister referred to "beating swords into ploughshares," and paid tribute to the tough, resourceful, stubborn man whose quiet dedication to his farming belied the passion he felt for his life. "Johnny would not have described himself as gentle, yet that hard strength of his was always in the service of a gentle spirit. That strength enabled him to treat those around him with a gentle hand . . ."

Al glanced around the room at the sunburnt faces

of a dozen farmers, nodding and avoiding eye contact. This description of Johnny could have been written for any one of them.

Swords into ploughshares, Al repeated to himself. Swords into ploughshares. And 'they that take the sword shall perish with the sword.' Johnny took the ploughshare, and every other piece of farm equipment that crossed his path. He took those machines and tools, used them, fixed them, redesigned and rebuilt them. He could operate any machine like a trained pro, given a half an hour of just looking at the thing. Johnny took the ploughshare and perished with the ploughshare.

He may not have died happily, but he died appropriately.

The minister was trying to sum up Johnny's life. Born in the area. Lived most of his life on the family farm. A brief stint in the Air Force at the end of the war, too near the end of it to see action. Continued to farm to his last day.

The end.

It was a life that Al could have chosen for himself. But he hadn't. In a way, he hadn't really chosen the life he was living. A couple of unfocused years of college after high school, an impulsive choice to drop out and move to Vancouver. His hours in the basement with his guitar and bass paid off with a paying gig from his first audition, and more than ten years of playing in anonymous bar bands. He had pretty much stumbled into it.

Some people never stumble into anything. Some make very deliberate choices; some are simply born into a life, or a destiny. Al considered that for Johnny it was probably equal portions of both. It was like Johnny had chosen to be born into his life as a farmer.

Although Al was born into a farming family, he doubted he would have chosen that, at least as a kid. The farm was an uneasy fit for him. There were things about it all that he always had trouble with. He had a hard time building up the calluses necessary for the work, at least the internal ones. Of course, his father was a bit that way too. There were things that his father had had a hard time with. If there was a dead calf, it had always been Al's job to bury the carcass. The smell was too much for his father, reminding him of his time in Europe during the war.

It wasn't handling dead animals that had soured Al on farming. He could handle that part of it fairly well. It was harder for him to deal with the maimed than with the dead or dying. He remembered finding a calf that had had its tail bitten off by a coyote. The calf survived, but Al felt a more visceral reaction to the amputation, the dismemberment, than he had to death. The risks to limbs or fingers in using power tools and farm machinery scared the hell out of him in those days.

He had built up the calluses on his fingertips, running them endlessly up and down the metal strings of his instruments. Few things make any more sense to a teenager than playing guitars for hours in a basement

room. Other things start making sense over time, things that seem dull and passionless when you're not quite ready to wear the title *adult*.

Eventually you can look at the life of an old bachelor farmer with understanding and a touch of envy.

Al was staring at the coffin as the minister gestured for everyone to stand. He recited a standard prayer, then stepped closer to address Johnny in his coffin:

"The eternal God is your dwelling place,

and underneath are the everlasting arms."

And the people said, "Amen."

Al whispered his Amen, his throat dry and his eyes tearless.

• • •

After a funeral, even work clothes don't feel comfortable. The daily routines are awkward, and although life goes on, it does so with a limping stride.

The harvest went on. It didn't feel wrong to Al to

get back on the tractor. If anything, it was a fitting tribute to Johnny to fire up the engines and get the machines rolling again. But this time, Al was climbing onto Johnny's tractor. He was starting up the stacker. Being the youngest dog, it was his place to learn the new tricks.

Al's uncle never had the patience to learn to operate the stacker.

◆ ◆ ◆

Al knew how the stacker was supposed to work. He'd watched it many times, worked on fixing it, listened to the stories about it. He spent the night before his maiden flight on the thing reading the manual. Now that he was starting to roll out and aim for the first row of bales lying in the field, he felt more nervous than he had at any audition.

The loading went pretty well. He started off in third gear, then went up to fourth as he gained confidence. He knew that Johnny had always used fifth or even sixth gear. That would come with time. Al stopped after the fourth layer went up into the rack; he pulled the lever to reset the machine for the tie layer. The two spikes extended up through the main table. Johnny had died while restacking the bales on the tie layer.

Al soon had a full load, his first. It took him just over half an hour. Johnny could do it in less than fifteen minutes. Now all he had to do was back it up to the stack and unload it.

It was not actually possible to see the stack behind the fully loaded hay rack. Al had to read peripheral clues to back the thing up to the existing stack, and spent another half hour going back and forth in low gear trying to line up the machine and the stack. He hopped down countless times to walk back and look at how far to the right or the left he needed to shift the thing. Finally, and it probably involved more luck and persistence than skill, Al had it where he wanted it. He climbed onto the tractor and pulled forward to swing the load up against the stack. He pulled the lever to extend the push-off feet and shove the machine and tractor away from the stack. He pulled away from the stack, reset the machine, and throttled down. He got down to check on the results.

When he had pulled forward to swing up the load, it turned out, he had pulled too far forward. A number of bales had fallen back into the gap between the load and the rest of the stack, then were squeezed awkwardly in between.

It was a mess.

To fix it would involve tearing down the stack by

hand and building it back up again.

Al looked at it and swore quietly. Then he swore loudly. He swore many more times, and dropped to his knees and swore some more. He beat his fists against a bale and swore. He swore at the stack, at the machine, at God, at himself, at the sky, at the machine again, at whoever. His uncle had driven up by this time, but he left Al alone to scream at the stack. He waited until Al was quiet and still and wiping the tears away.

"Well, the first stack is always for learning," he said. "It's a hell of a trick, doing it right. Johnny'd been at it long enough to make it look easy. Your first stack is pretty much a sacrifice. You gotta do it so you can do it better the next time." He picked up one of the eighty-pound bales and tossed it out of the way to start the process of rebuilding the stack.

Al got up and joined him. After spreading out about thirty bales, he said, "What was Johnny's first stack like? Anything like this?"

Sutherland stopped and looked down the straight line of the stack, Johnny's last stack. "Hell, no," he said. "Johnny's first stack was perfect. A thing of beauty." Al laughed. Sutherland went on. "It was just like in the manual. Of course, Johnny improved on the manual's instructions, sent a letter to the manu-facturer the next day." Al flopped down onto a bale to laugh silently. "Of course," Sutherland continued, "he couldn't play guitar to save his life."

• • •

Al's next load was about the same as his first. After rebuilding it, he went out to start his third.

ACKNOWLEDGEMENTS

I would like to thank the following: The Cochrane Coffee Traders and the Auburn Saloon, for the moral and chemical support; the (now defunct) Western Heritage Centre for sponsoring the Write 'em Cowboy Short Story Contest, which put some money in my pocket for the story "Succession," and brought me to the attention of Brindle & Glass; the backstage community of Calgary's music and theatre scenes for the interest and support; the musicians, theatre artists and writers of Victoria and Vancouver from my bohemian days in the eighties; Barnabas for the spiritual home; my family, especially my parents, for this piece of land where I farm and write; "Stagger" Lee Shedden, my editor and guru; and, of course, Molly.

Art Norris was born the day after the assassination of JFK. The two events appear to be unrelated.

He was raised on a dairy farm near Calgary, Alberta. He went on to study at the University of Victoria and earned a BFA in Theatre. He enjoyed several years of bohemian obscurity in Victoria, earning money with farm work, tree planting and daffodil harvesting while working away at music and writing. As the guitar-playing half of Impolite Company, Art wrote music for a small pile of satirical songs, some of which made it to CBC Radio's comedy syndication. Notably, their song "Hockey Nut in Canada" was played between periods at Vancouver Canucks home games during their playoff series oh-so-long-ago.

In the late eighties, Art opted for the stability of a career in the professional performing arts. He has worked as a stage carpenter, lighting technician, stage manager and technical consultant in theatres and concert venues in Victoria, Vancouver, Edmonton and Calgary, where he now is a stage manager and stage carpenter at the Jack Singer Concert Hall.

Art lives with his wife and son on the family farm near Calgary, raising organic beef cattle.